Cori and the Hidden World

Cori and the Hidden World

DLC: Clavis' Capers

Urie Wilson

Copyright Info

LCCN: 2024924168
Paperback: ISBN: 979-8-9891283-5-8
Ebook: ISBN: 979-8-9891283-4-1

Dedication

This is formerly a love letter to all media history, but I found out that I can do better and make bigger waves than everything saying that I couldn't. And I am still missing a lot of friends and/or family members. So, if anything happens, I'm sorry but I am not. Tee hee, *smiles*

I give thanks to my family, who says all the time that they said they couldn't tell their family members that they can't be what they want to be for a job, my gut and its instincts for being proof that I saved them and the real version of my dream self, who stood up for me at times and told me that he doesn't have to be any bigger a superstar than he actually is...

Table of Contents

Reading Hints

As you can see, the author tried to his best to put the story into a format that is fitting for literature standards to have the feel of a professionally published book, fantasy standards to be read like a fairy tale, video game standards to make blueprints of the author's future works and biblical standards to avoid religious conflict completely as possible. All conflict related to this afterward is purely coincidental and doesn't mean the author knows about it nor its coexistence yet.

The story has two fictional barriers made to not become real: the actual time it occurred and the status of its existence. It is in the form of a play, so the author expects you to act like you're in a game with play narratives while the narrator is telling the story and imagine that you know what the characters in the play look like.

The author also recommends that you have a very good IQ level and read Cori and the Hidden World and all of its content before reading this first...or make up an original story with the characters in this one before doing it.

Characters

CAPTAIN NEON N. CARD – a ruthless, notorious leader of the Card Pirates looking for what he calls the ultimate treasure to rule Dreamia

FIRST MATE RAS T. FELT – a sleazy, devilish First Mate of Captain Neon who's a high-achieving, beautiful menace

QUARTERMASTER MARY P. MAYWHEATHER – a kid twin Card Pirate Quartermaster sister of Shelly who's smart and cutthroat

QUARTERMASTER SHELLY U. MAYWHEATHER – a kid twin Card Pirate Quartermaster sister of Mary who's not so bright but a screwball

BUCCANEER CLAVIS EDGEY – an intuitive dreamer of a Level 5 Card Pirate Buccaneer of a very high rank leading his own squadron

GUNNER GROTTOLY GOLDS – a surly, experienced and grumpy Level 20 Card Pirate Gunner of a very high rank leading his own squadron

TRAPPER FIBA CHOCOLATTE – a somewhat fickle Level 5 Card Pirate Trapper of a very high rank leading her own squadron

WEAPONMASTER PEEP LYLES – an extremely high-level Card Pirate Weaponmaster of a very high rank leading his own squadron who takes care of the S.S. Nutting per Captain Neon's orders to grind experience in his spare time

WITCH DOCTOR DJ FLANK – an extremely high-level Card Pirate Witch Doctor DJ wearing his own celeb DJ gear that's training under Captain Neon as Captain Neon's top secret scheme

THE MYSTERIOUS KIDS? - The three kids that mysteriously wandered into O' Dee Tee Town and suddenly attacked the Card Pirates while it was being plundered by them

THE WACKY INFLATABLE RUBBER TUBE TREE – a lonely, wacky tree that doesn't seem lively, but moves along with the steam it's rooted above

THE TIMONKEY? - a half-tiger, half-gorilla boss Mun who is terrorizing Semi Cotta Jungle

Main Story

Theater Prologue

Hello! Welcome to Hathaway Theater! I'm Collin, the manager. Boy, do we have a story to tell you! Ever thought how much money illegally goes into villainy? What about how far the apple rots from the tree? Or why people ask often about how an airplane flies or why the sky is blue in response to being asked vital questions?

In a world full of evil, it's often too dangerous to go alone. But these pirates have two things with them while being multiple battalions in one crew: a worldwide treasure hunt and a game plan. As insufferable as they came in on, you will find out the answers to the questions that I just asked you as they prove why they were once the most feared evil on earth. Without further ado, enjoy the show.

Hi! Clavis' the name. And you'd better remember me! Because I don't see you risking you lives keelhauling explosive barrels, or being instructed or betrayed past your life, or running a multi-million-dollar video game company...wait a minute, hold that thought, let's put it all behind us, okay?

As I heard the news, my former captain and his crew had been defeated by a ragtag team of kids. Probably took their loved ones or something. Well I wouldn't want to cross them in mind. Still, it's a good thing that "@&:++(-) captain had it really coming to him! I guess I owe it to them for putting my fears to rest. Also, you for knowing about them. What!? You hear about them everyday, here!?!? These kids aren't ordinary. Maybe they're with a superhero group, or that man upstairs everyone's been talking about...still can't afford to mess up my life on the spot, anyway.

That girl with that robo-thingy she's engaged with looks mighty familiar…

I'm well settled, now, heehee. *smiling* Want to hear my story? Here's how it all started…

Chapter 1: Much Ado About Nutting

There was a loud explosion on the northern hemisphere of Dreamia, as I so now thought the planet was called. The whole crew was leaving on their airship. The captain was seen laughing his tail off and his top mates were celebrating with him. "Well, that was something!!!!" Then he turned to that Jezebel demon of a mate called Ras T. Felt, was it? And said, "Ras, Status Report!" And she was alluring like, "300 packages were loaded, killed 20 survivors and let off 4 personnel." The captain was guffawing afterwards wiping a tear of joy from his right eye, then said, "You! Mary! Shelly! The packages!" As aloof as she came by, Mary said, "So far, most of them are minor key and recovery items, but we have a few museum documents, these ones are a big buzz!," and the smart one, Shelly, I ought to throw a turtle shell a her, says, "Talk about bee-ing supercharged!" "Let me see!," the captain said as he collected the papers and began sorting them out. "A new battery-powered engine, might do later, some universal handyman tools, never, I got my own, *gibberish, gibberish...*" And as he found the paper, the very paper that would change our lives forever, he says, "...all-powerful relic... what!?...this device has to do with the fabled Dev Heck of

Dreamia. Legendary rumor says that if it's activated at the fifth basement floor of Dev Heck it would grant anyone who activated it immeasurable power!" His top mates gathered around him as all of them were amazed. What? My talking's now formal all of a sudden? Well, what else do you expect with that kind of moment? Back to the story, "Mates, this is the pinnacle of all pinnacles!" Then Mary goes, " I wonder what kind of powers we might get with that, I want to grow up with the boy of my dreams," Shelly goes, "Well, I want the power to speak to animals," and Ras was like, "Well I want to make my lips and butt even bigger….," and he was like, "Wait your turn, you mermaids! No one said I was going to share it, nor it can be shared with anyone else! I'll get the power and see if I can share it with you!" The mates celebrated with that quote and you know what? Good luck with that, because I didn't see what happened a few pages and chapters later coming, either!

I heard it all. I was a Card Pirate buccaneer seeing and listening to them from a grill in the floor of the top level of the ship right above the barracks, where I usually hang out before doing anything. I was a Card Pirate Buccaneer, 543rd Class, about to go up to 486th Class, Level 5. Sitting beside me sleeping was Grottoly, 358th Class Card Pirate Gunner, Level 20, and Fiba, well wouldn't you know, 486th Class Card Pirate Trapper, Level 10. So, I said, "Wow, I don't believe my ears! Sounds like something that'll treat something right like a very good lady… imagine what it might do if it was fully shared!" Then Grottoly, as all old-like, told me, "What are you talking about, Clavis?" See? I'm good with conversations, too, you know… So Fiba replied, "Is this another treasure anticipation thing you've holding up? It's been the 80th week!!!" Oh, how do I do this, right, "Doesn't mean he didn't bring anything good out of it," said the grumpy gun user. If you'd ever address that line in front of him, he'd kill you. I'm dead serious! Enough with the jokes, let's get on to the screen play. And he was right! So, I broke up the possible fight that was going to happen because of me and said, "Guys, stop it! This the moment we could be waiting for!!! I bet that could turn around our lives! Say, Grottoly, when did you ever want to be known for your age?" And Grottoly answers, "And repeat a scene from a famous book and another one about Middle Earth?" I asked Fiba next. "Fiba, you've always wanted to date..a…real person, and not a victim, right?" Fiba then asks, "Who asked you, Cupid?," and then a one-sided fight breaks out, until one of the Card Pirate Gunmasters yells, "Hey! Break it up, there's a briefing at two, better show up," and he threw our clean clothes on the floor as if it were nothing, and we stopped fighting as we heard the news!

So at two, Grotto, Fiba and I arrived at the usual spot, the large supply room next to the barracks, and attended our next briefing. All the other pirates were there. Mary shouted out loud, "ALRIGHT, YOU ANIMALS!!!! OUR CAPTAIN HAS SOMETHING TO SAY!!!!!!," and steps aside for the Captain to speak… "Thank you, Mary," he said. And as a member was about to say something as he was about to step up, he made a step, quickly took his rastfelt out and shot him dead in an instant! "What? You wanted to say something!?," he went on. "Aren't you actually welcome in our crew?" And he pointed his gun out to another person that flinched in the audience. That guy had his arms held up in fear. "What about you?," the Captain went. The guy he stuck up nods yes. Next, the Captain aims his gun at more members. "What about you? Or you? Or you!? Or you, for that matter!?," he went. Then he suddenly slammed his arms on the desk and went, "WHY PUT MY FUN AT RISK!?!?!? Try me if you dare!!!! Here is what I am going to do…" Now, he puts a map through a projector and shuts almost every light in the ship off. "We go to this toy box of a village on Country A where there's an in-depth copy of a document we found from the post office." The Captain swaps out the map with said document, yatta, yatta, all that about, zzz…huh? Where was I? So he says, "So, if anyone sees something similar to this document, bring it to the ship immediately!" He shows himself and his top leads just to point out what he'll do next in the nasty plot. "We will be going to their mayor's meeting to have a little talk with them…heeheehee, hee…*guffaws* MEETING OVER!!!!"

After the meeting, everyone went back to their own business. Some of the other crew members began to talk about what my ragtag group has been talking about. I, on the other hand, kept a tight lip and didn't say anything, because if I said anything while clamoring over that document, and well, I'd be shot. Peep, one of Gunmasters that broke up my fight with Grottoly and Fiba just as I was about to get creamed, then called me, like, "Ay, you! The Captain has something ready for a few of you," and then pushes me up to the deck with the other four. I hope it's not a bullet to the face!

So there we are. Me, Grottoly, Fiba and another guy, a Level 20 pirate of a new kind, called a Card….Pirate..Witch…doctor…DJ, sporting track gear, white sneakers, a fake gold chain, guess he can't get anymore famous, and a skull-and-cards-themed helmet, named, and get this: Flank. Now, I bet you all were going on all sorts of adventures with him, haha! Where was I, oh, right, so the Captain was far away in his cabin. The whole deck was now made into a training ground. Peep now goes to its door and knocks. "What is it?," said Mr. Gooeythunderpants. "They're all here, captain!," replied Peep. The Captain comes out. Now, I bet this sounds like a scary movie moment, right? He says, "*inhales* I KNOW YOU ALL ARE FRUSTRATED WITH EACH OTHER, COME ON OUT WITH IT!!!!!!" "Got a power level over 9000, I'll kill your azz!," said to me by an angry Grotto.

I said, "Said to you by your 9000 moms!" Fiba asks Flank, "What's this guy in all that getup?" Then Flank angrily says, "Off me, you little shipbox! Can't you see I got a show to run?" If he was a major Thumb Tanks movie villain, let me know! "I'll give you a show!," says Fiba, and before a fight even breaks out, the Captain yells, "ALRIGHT!!! CUT IT OUT!!!!!! Listen…I picked all of you here for an important job. You're the finest of my crew the whole world feared other than my Quartermasters and First Mate! Here's what I want you to do…you're going to learn how to lead while working together – making a task force making task forces!" The Captain points out to me, Grotto and Fiba. He says, "The three of you!," and comes closer. Then as unexpected, he fights the living heck out of us while pointing out each major flaw of us while being unquestioned. "What the duck is the matter with you? Can't you see there's a world waiting for you? What's the matter? Can't wait to pull out of a good argument? And what's this with you? Got rabid fever?" As he stopped, he began to say as he pulls out his gun, "There! Now, are we settled, eh…*locks and loads pistol, holds it in air*" We forcefully set aside all differences and agreed. "Well, now…," the Captain says while slapping his knee. "Here's the thing…" He points out to all of us. "We're all following the rules of us being Munnons on this planet!" He points out to the three of us again. "You three are all Tules!" He then points to Flank. "This guy is a Sownd and a Tule!" He points out to Peep. "The Meem Tule already got his briefing done." Peep nods with his arms folded, saying, "And I know that, for one…" And the Captain comes out to me. "You're a buccaneer, right?" I nodded a yes. Then he comes at me fighting me and saying, "Show me what you got!"

He blocked my sword moves. I countered every move. He shot at me and I cut away every bullet in half and to a halt. "Remember, a buccaneer is the best sword fighting henchman in every fiction. You'd better live up to it!," he said. Tell me he meant fake books. You can tell me that it's not real! The fight went on. "You're going to have think harder from here!," the Captain went. As I dodged his attacks, which became more fox-worthy, I cut into the floor around him as I took my turns. Then in one of them, he took a step into his usual planning spot and fell into the hole I cut around him that he broke into and the fight ended. "What the…AHHHHHHH!," he went. So many wents, I'll spruce it up a bit…

The Captain now climbs out of the hole I made laughing, saying, "That was a good one!" He slammed his left arm on a side of the hole with a thumbs up from it towards me. He finishes laughing and faces Grotto. "Alright, you're next!" And then he climbs out of the hole, walks towards him and then fights him.

Grotto shoots several shots into the Captain, but the Captain didn't make a move until he said before he makes his turn, "See anything different?," while raising his arms and suddenly attacks Grotto, as the gunner is now dodging the Captain's sword attacks and gun fire. "The gunner is supposed to be the most sly and bravest one of the group! Take your chances, whippersnapper!," the Captain went. And Grotto, as bad as he gets, starts thinking of equipping fatal-shot equipment and hiding in the middle of battle, and it worked. Here's how: every turn he got, he threw small bottles of liquor in front of the Captain, threw gunpowder on it and lit it ablaze, and while the Captain was almost able to catch up with him, he took the chance to load his gun with trinkets from past members that he now sacrificed to make more deadly fire and hits the Captain hard! And the Captain was sent far back across the deck!

As the Captain got up from the deck floor, he said, "That's was a good one!" Next, he says to Fiba, "Now, onto you!," walks towards her as she prepares her traps with his sword in tow and starts running towards her. Let me tell you the most interesting battle to date…

She throws a chained bear trap through him from between his legs and starts setting up more bear traps, this time laced with gravity sensors that bring down and helps to ensnare the foe, right in front of the Captain as he uses his sword to set off in front of him trap after trap and making big shock waves to send off waves of them while Fiba is still yanking the first trap's chain while running from him. "The trap master needs to stay light on their feet if she wants to dodge this monster! Keep it up!," he said. Then she witnessed that most of her traps, the gravity-sensor-laced ones, had a long term effect, as they put a few pounds on the Captain and his weaponry, causing him to slowly lose them, and she lays out 10 more of them in front, runs away, walls away with a dream powder cloud, runs away, puts 30 more traps in front and runs to the front of the deck. She sends spike arrow traps with her bow to the sides the Captain would run to to dodge the bear traps and the dream powder cloud so that he would have nothing but to run forward and catch her. And before you know it, he loses his sword to the traps and runs forward to take out his gun and shoot, but the dream powder flies up his nose and he gets very drowsy, tips forward, falls asleep, lands on the traps and gets snapped on repeatedly. That battle ended terrifically!

We waited for the Captain to wake up after the whole thing. As we cleaned up and he recovered, he goes, *snort* "Where was I? Oh, yeah!," And he inspects the area and himself, goes to Fiba, pats her on the back and says to her, "Good one, if I say so, myself!," and lays off her. He then yells, "OKAY, FELLAS! YOU KNOW HOW TO GET PAST ME! BUT WHAT ABOUT THIS ONE?," and points out to Flank. "MIND YOUR ONE-LINERS!" He begins to call Flank. "FLANK, GET OVER

HERE!" Flank comes over to him. "Give them front row tickets to a premier of your handy work!" "Yes, Captain!," said Helmethead. And he starts the battle with all three of us!

As Flank makes his first turn he prepares his equipment while saying, "And just so you know,... there's a reason why you should respect my drip...," and he plays a sick beat for a moment. And the next thing you know, I was mind controlled into attacking my crew mates every turn! Fiba and Grotto didn't believe it, either, as Grotto was downed and Fiba was questioning Flank on what he did as she took her turn to free me from his control, as he replied, "Or else!," and makes his turn by using his turntable to keep track of our party's side effects by emitting a... graphical...display...of a music staff with some notes dressed like us on it from his mix table, makes an artificial note looking like her, puts her on the staff and paralyzes her as she is now suspended in midair, arms down! As we struggled to free ourselves, he gets turn after turn whittling our health away as he witch-doctored us to near death until some of us broke free, and get this, I don't blame the world for trying, but it's such an angel at the knife, so what I was saying, is we somehow freed ourselves thanks to our limits of getting status effects in layers, and you know what happens, next? He sends an electric pulse to the staff line where Fiba is and it closes in on it from both sides, crashing into it, splitting it open, destroying it and killing her, I break free and the display disappeared, but it was too late to make my turn, as Grotto makes his turn shooting Flank up, which had no effect, since he was overpowered for his level, and Flank's staff lines appeared again, only that he sticks a few needles into a note dressed like Grotto, sends it to the staff, hurting Grotto very much, ends his turn, I make my turn cutting the mix table in two, but he mends it perfectly together again via mysterious beat boxing, Grotto attempts dent Flank greatly with critical shots, but managed to take 10HP off of him, Flank blares his turn away with a sick beat again and witch-doctored us to death, as he said, "Get rotated!"

As the Captain revives me, Grotto and Fiba with some Deep Miracles, he says, "See this one? He's my ace in the hole should something happen to me…try to catch up with him for me!," yells, "MEETING OVER! BACK TO YOUR STATIONS! This guy is coming with me for some private training…" and leaves with Flank into his cabin.

Me, Grotto and Fiba went to our bedrooms and began to have a good night's rest. Our home airship, the S.S. Nutting began to sail for Country B. I should tell more bedtime stories…zzz… what?

Chapter 2: The Attack of Walawalaville

Let me get this…as the S.S. Nutting flies into Country A territory, it makes a crash stop in Walawalaville. Sounds like a news report is going to air…lots of us stormed out of the ship into the village, plundering and killing. As for my team, we led groups of the same types as us. And look at that! There's love in the air, already! Mary and Shelly were fighting over a kid that they wanted to make theirs! And Ras just wooed a person into being killed by her! What a darn shame…and as the Captain walked into the Walawalaville town building, the heads of the town were just talking about which district leader would claim something.

Here's what I was told...

He gets in front of everyone by cutting a map pawn in half, dragging his sword and a large part of the map to his position and saying, "And this part of the land belongs to me!!!" A district member tries to correct him. Well, I'm just telling you what the other guy said…"That's not how you m-" And the

Captain slashes him to death. The other district members were wondering what he's doing there as he tells the slain member, "Be quiet! I know when I should take my turn!," and then to the others, "Isn't that how we should do things here?" The guys were all confused and scared. I can know the feeling. "Say, where is the manager I can report to?," he coined. And as one of the leaders reaches for a gun on the shelf, that leader says to him, "...right....HERE!!!," grabs and wields it, and one of the bloodiest battles in Walawalaville begins...

The leader shoots at the Captain, the Captain deflect the bullet at another leader killed by it, the other leaders grab their guns and start firing at their missed pirate captain target with some shots gotten in, as it didn't stop the Captain, who slashes some of them dead with his sword, gets into brawls with the rest until he uses his weapon to go for the kill on the rest of them and says, "Bad customer service..."

By the time I was through, the whole village was being destroyed and catching fire. What did I do? Killed a few cross-region armies, plundered many residential areas and stole a TV! What the heck are you looking at me like that for? It was the Captain's orders! Then the Captain came out of the town's treasury with another document! Guess what this one is...it was the one to narrow down the treasure hunt! As Grotto, Fiba and my squads were done and regrouping, more of our crew were still plundering. Then the Captain said, "Okay, fellas, follow me...," and we boarded the airship and took off.

As the S.S. Nutting sails across the sky, all the crew had a meeting. "*Guffaws* We had a great time, there!," said Captain Babyfoot as he led the convo. Mind your own darn grammar! "And with a stroke of luck, we have the document!" And he gets all emotional and points his sword out at the watching crew with his feelings out. "And it comes to just show you, that if you keep fighting for what you believe in, you may actually get something good coming your way!" I suppose me, Grotto, Fiba and everyone else in the whole dang crew gets a puppy, too. Next, he says, "Quarters, status report!" "*Sob*I didn't get anything, Shelly broke my boy toy!," cried Mary. "*Sob*No, I didn't! You stole him from me!," cried Shelly. Oh, bother…the argument went on until the Captain said, "SHUT IT, BOTH OF YOU!," takes a random member out in the open, stands back and points his sword out at him while he's quaking in fear and says while gesturing, "... because if I hear one little peep of frustration out of you when he leaves, then I'LL END IT FOR BOTH OF YOU!" "Yaaaaaaaaaayyyyyyy!," said the twins as they carried their next victim off. I don't know if that was lucky, to be honest…then the Captain points out to Ras. "You there, what happened?" "I caught a glimpse of a bunch of jazz instruments from a pic of some dude that caught my eye. Sounds like he's married to someone with a set of lungs on her…," she said. "Good, Ras. Now we know where to hit next for our coronation's band members' instruments!," said the Captain. One problem with that: I hate flutes! Then the Captain points out to one of his Weaponmasters and says, "You there, what happened?" The Weaponmaster said, "All the Gunmasters and Swordmasters are loaded and ready to begin their training." "Excellent," said the Captain. Look, keep up, okay? And then he points out to his strongest squads and says, "And you, there! Status report!" We reported our squads' activities to him. It's us he was talking to, after all. He liked how I soloed Walawalaville's armies. He couldn't help but haul away some of my plundering. Grotto got into it with some of his men. Fiba ran around in circles trying to make each of her traps work. Hey, this is the part where she'd accidentally run into some of them. He says, "Good, as long as you keep pirating!," and then says, "Get some rest, all of you! It's going to be a long day ahead.

CLASS DISMISSED!!!!" We sailed for the HapTV Studio on Country B to drop off Ras. I got into my room to watch the Handyman horror movie until my squad leader ca padres decided to fight me over the chills I would get from it upon watching it at night. We fell asleep afterward as the ship was halfway towards Plus Isle.

Chapter 3: Let the Games Begin!

As the S.S. Nutting was halfway towards Country B, it was morning. All the Weaponmasters, Gunmasters and Swordmasters were cleaning it, with special orders from the Captain. A lemony scent woke me up a little, but but my sleep was undeterred. Until I heard a loud vacuum noise accompanied by a, "Wake up, it's morning! Wake up! Wake up! Get up and get ready for breakfast!," from one of the Weaponmaster pirates. Like, I already have an alarm clock, here! Who are you, my mom? So I did. Everyone had a plate they can eat anywhere. But today was no ordinary day. It was Saturday, the day I would play one of my favorite games: Barrel Stacker! So I ate and went to the ship's cargo bay, where the crew was setting the game up.

There was master after master, setting up barrel after barrel, on top of each other. They were randomizing barrel setups by switching out random ones with ones that counted as good or bad power-ups. The stacks were dead set up to rise as the barrels that were set in stacks of two just waiting to be destroyed. As the game was fully set up, the Captain rushed to the area saying, "Great, my favorite game!," got word that everything was all good to go and got everyone's attention with a spoon and an empty pot as they gathered to him. "Listen up! Welcome to today's Barrel Stacker tourney!," said the old lion mouth. "Peep, explain the rules!"

Next, Peep yells as he began to explain. "THE RULE OF THE GAME IS TO DESTROY THE BARRELS ON YOUR SIDE UNTIL EITHER OF YOU COULDN'T ANYMORE FIRST. IF YOU CAN'T, YOU LOSE THE GAME AND THE OTHER SIDE WINS. THERE ARE 4 TYPES OF BARRELS. THE CAUCASIAN ONES ARE THE STANDARD ONES. THEY BREAK WITH EASE AND IN GROUPS. THE RED ONES EXPLODE WHEN TOUCHING ANY GROUP NEXT TO IT. THE GREEN ONES SPRING PUNCHING ARMS CROSS-WISE. GOOD FOR TAKING OUT JUNK CRATES AND NEARBY RED BARRELS. THE YELLOW BARRELS STRIKE WITH LIGHTNING BOLTS GOING VERTICALLY. IF YOU COMBINE TWO OR MORE OF THE SAME BARREL, THEY COMBINE TO MAKE A CRATE. THE BIGGER THE COMBINATION, THE BIGGER THE CRATE! DESTROY A BIG CRATE OF A CERTAIN KIND AND GET A BIGGER KIND OF EFFECT. THE BIGGEST CRATE DESTROYED HAS THE BIGGEST EFFECT. IF YOU DESTROY A CRATE, YOU SEND A JUNK CRATE DEPENDING ON ITS SIZE TO DROP ON TOP OF THE OTHER PLAYER'S STACK. THE BIGGEST CRATE DESTROYED SENDS THE BIGGEST JUNK CRATE! THE STACK WILL SLOWLY RISE FASTER OVER TIME. ACCIDENTS CAN HAPPEN. YOU CAN ACCIDENTALLY SEND A POWERFUL JUNK CRATE TO THE OTHER SIDE. YOU CAN ALSO COMBINE CRATES, BUT ONLY OF EQUAL HEIGHT OR WIDTH." "Get all of this?

You won't see anything like this on this world!," the Captain said. He raised his right arm. "Are you ready?" After a few minutes he quickly chops downward with it and says, "Start! How about you, here?" And picks two players and starts the game.

We took turns playing Barrel Stacker. There were winners and losers. It was a matter of being the last one standing. When it came to the Captain's turn, he was taking out the winners in the game with mad game-playing skills. When it came to my turn, I was up against him. I beat all the players up to this point. "This person, here…," he went. And we clashed.

We were the top players on the ship, trading junk crate after junk crate, taking out barrel after barrel, using every power-up ever. I let him strike the first power-up crate and send it on top of my stack, but I followed up with a few hefty junk crate combos and waited for him. The minute the stacks were ripe for combos, we hurried to give each other wrenches to each other's plans, but my quick thinking kept the stacks short, kept him occupied and sent a flurry of crate stacks for the finish. Mwahahahahaha!!!!!!!!!!!! What? I finally got the old custard!

Anyway, he says, "Oh, my gosh! *guffaws* That was a good one! Let's drop off Ras." So he did. I didn't know she was running a win streak in the Nightmian Monster Hunt league. And as the crew was chased off back into the ship, we left for Whipped Dreamland on Country A to drop her off again. It was noon. After everyone was well rested, there was another meeting. It was about tomorrow's plans. "Greetings, gentlemen! As soon as tomorrow morning, we'll drop off Ras at Whipped Dreamland and prepare for the main event with another mission afterward. Now I know she's celebrating her victory as Nightmian Monster Hunt league champion, and we love her very much…MIND YOU, SHE IS NOT SOME BACKYARD TRAILER TRASH!!!!," the Captain said and he shoots a few crew members dead. And none of the squad leaders were harmed, whatsoever. He yells at a Weaponmaster pirate. "STATUS REPORT!!!!!!" "All Weaponmasters, Gunmasters and Swordmasters are halfway through their training, captain," the poor guy said. "Good. Peep, is everything clean?," the Captain went on to Peep. "So good, you can eat off of it, captain," said Peep. "Goooood, it's time I slapped some sense into these sex-crazed hooligans!" We go through another projector slideshow as he explains. There was what I think is some man's family photo shown at the moment. "At noon, we attack O' Dee Tee Town. Living instruments are we? If so, I know what to do with the Bagpipes!" He shows a slide of a drawing of us plundering, then a slide of a drawing of a pile of musical instruments and then a slide of the whole crew in royal gear while he's in the middle in king gear and the rest of the Quartermasters in royal gear. "We'll plunder all of them for their instruments to prepare for our coronation. Any questions?" The place went silent for a few seconds. Then he complained with gestures, "I know we are going through some tough times, but I got to admit..." Then a crew member came out and yelled with his arms wide open and in the air, "I know, but we already know the full plan...," and the Captain got angry and said, "So, you think you know better than me!?," and the guy replied in disagreement. The Captain then aimed at him with his gun and said, "Do you really mean it!?!?!" The guy was pleading for his life in agreement! In freaking agreement!!!!! "Good enough," the Captain said as he put his weapon away. "Class dismissed!!!" I think that guy's nerves were wrecked out of his body. Everyone went to their quarters trying to shake off the confusion. I went to sleep and all of a sudden had the best dream ever. I know I'm a bad guy, but some of the most interesting things good guys get can also happen to us. I dreamed that I was signing a contract to make games at a game company, and one of my best selling games was a video game version of Barrel Stacker, and at the end of it, I was laughing and being rich with all the money surrounding me. Then I woke up at the morning feeling fine. "Guys, do you think I can make a killing with a video game?," I asked Grotto and Fiba. "I don't know, but I suppose one off of Barrel Stacker. Why?," answered my gun-mastering friend. "No one has did it before!," said Fiba. "Then, that's it! I'm going to do it!," I declared. "What!!? The code will kill you!," said Grotto and Fiba said, "The work costs thousands of dollars!" Then I said, "So what, I've got the know-how, and the drawing skills in order to make the game, so read it and weep! My mind's made up, and I'm not going to let home stop me!" So I grabbed a backpack, lots of paper, a few drawings pens and started making my schematics for it as the S.S. Nutting sails toward Whipped Dreamland. Near the time we were there, the notes were complete. Later we dropped Ras off and sailed towards O' Dee Tee Town for our next mission.

Chapter 4: Ambushed Plunder at O' Dee Tee

Upon the S.S. Nutting firing as shot at one of O' Dee Tee Town's largest buildings and temporarily parking in the wreckage to unload a major of the crew, the Captain bolted out of the cargo bay with his sword out, pointed it towards the town and shouted, "ALL 3 MILLS, STORM THE TOWN!!!!!," and my, Grotto and Fiba's squads went out on the attack as the airship took off with the rest.

We stormed until all of the squad leaders were far ahead of their squads. Then I looked to the back of me while I was plundering and killing, and saw that three kids, a pinkish-farm-getup-wearing black kid, a purple-bodied, purple-fedora-wearing humanoid black mascot in his teens with a magic stick and an all-black-wearing blue haired, black priestess with a black priestess crown, enter the wreckage through the door of that building we wrecked. Is she a princess? I shrugged my arms and kept doing my business as I kept my eyes on them as they picked up one of the Captain's deadly playing card mementos from one of his victims. I joked in my head as I kept on going about them taking 25 minutes charging up and transforming into Class 1,000,000 anger-fueled, dead-avenging pee storms. Guess what happened next? It somewhat really happened.

They made some kind of teamwork handiwork, and the next thing you know, they began instantly killing wave after wave of me and my other main 2 squad leader companions' crews in a flash. I panicked and got the other leaders' attention at my hardest! And the trio's bee companion thing was being even cowardly in the middle of it!!! AND HE FREAKING TANKED!?!? We got the rest of our squads to retreat and follow us as we signaled the Captain to arrive! He called the ship to arrive further ahead of the direction were headed, outside of the town, and we filled the ship, leaving a lot of members for dead! And that's what killed the Captain!?!? From what I heard, okay…

Then as the trio were in the middle of the town with no butt to kick, the ship took off and the Captain rushed to their location and ambushed them! Like what I was told and like in their documentary, they have kept telling him to give up and surrender. My money's on the kids, but the Captain can make amendments, too. So he closes in on them and introduces himself to them as he gets close to them enough to fight the dog mess out of them. And the bug teen takes off crying like a beotch, leaving the other two to fight the Captain alone!!! Oh, those bloody kids!!! And they made him retreat while asking him to give up!!

As the Captain climbed the ladder to the airship, all I heard from within the barracks, now-turned-infirmary, "Remember my name from across this world's seven seas!!!!!" That's the worst chilling words you'll ever hear from a world-class pirate! Still, yet true…so the S.S. Nutting sailed towards a boundary between Error Four O' Four Forest and Semi Cotta

Jungle by their outer corners just to pick up Ras while we were still retreating to recuperate for the next attack. Next to that came-filled part of the sea! Can it get any worse? At least it's losing the "came" and "we die if we're near it" part!

The next day we held a meeting with the Captain in a wide open area. He brought a podium in front of him with restraint, and as soon as he inhaled, I knew that it was going to be something we all bloody didn't like.

The Captain then slammed both arms on the podium and said, "What was that?" A guy said, "I know, right?" "That's what I was waiting to hear!," the Captain said. What, I could relate with everyone on this! "Those kids must've been on drugs!," another crew member said. "Couldn't have been me!!!," the frustrated C went. "Did anyone steal from them?" A few went, "No," and, "No, captain!," and one went, "No one had the idea, captain!" "I was waiting for that, too!," the Captain went. "Well, you got any plans for them?," a member said to him. "You're taking the words right out of my mouth!," the Capta-eh, well, you know what was happening. Then he yelled in a rage, "WELL, SINCE YOU SASSY DELINQUENTS HAVE SOMETHING TO SAY, YOU'LL BE WITH ME ALL DAY!!! I EXPECT A STATUS REPORT FROM EVERY ONE OF YOU IN THE MORNING!!! LET'S CHOP IT UP!!!!"

And we picked up Ras from the amusement park, who was drunk off of root beer. But it wasn't easy, that clown kid leading a bunch of mutant cats was no joke, so don't ask me how it played out. Where was she during that time? I bet she was being used as an ace-in-the-hole for some grand scheme…I was talking about Ras, if you didn't know…

Chapter 5: A Chaotic Leave!

The man upstairs bless the almighty Urie Wilson for coming up with these chapter names, swell guy. Please get him some good friends! Because this event was where things were going to tick me off…

The next morning, each crew member came to the Captain with a status report. Let's see what each of them were…a lost crew member, a broken limb, some supply shortages, the works. And believe me, we were WORKED!!! I made a report, but upon hearing more details of how I promoted a successful retreat, he kicked me out of his cabin in a fury.

The S.S. Nutting took off in a hurry, but it floated in midair. The next thing, we were having a meeting with the Captain in the cargo bay and when I saw him after entering the room, he was talking with a member, saying something about no one can hear us. The room got dark, then shone a light on the Captain as he began to explain. "Okay, fellas, class is in session!," he let out. Oh, gosh, the slideshow started again! He shows a drawing of the stuff we took from O' Dee Tee Town, then a drawing of an injured, living and bleeding tuba in tears. "In this

lesson, while we didn't get what we needed from O' Dee Tee Town, we left them in stitches." He
 next showed drawings of recovery plans. This is all through the projector. "So, we sorted through the materials and found loads of electrical equipment to upgrade and recover our ship." A map of Country A with a power plant's coordinates on it was shown next. "So this is our next assignment!" He showed drawings of the mission, from staff and plant details, to operations done if they retaliate as he explained about them. "In the Zsip Power Plant is a crew working on the country's power while connected with several others across the globe using thunderclouds as an energy source, working on using dream clouds as energy, and working with a mythical crew of their company of a high rank called the Zsip Liners! I'd hate them, if they exist! That's when I'll be sending Mary and Shelly into the building. Right after saying hello! When I actually give their watchman the usual airship greeting! They won't suspect a thing…once this is over, they'll give me intel on the power plant, and we'll see what's inside as we rob the nation of its sweet little power grid that it's been holding onto, despite millions of TVs that it cheated on, Mwahahahahahaaaaaaaa! If you're selected by them, then you're helping them in the mission. CLASS DISMISSED!!!!!!!!!"

The meeting was wrapping up, when suddenly I went up to Fiba and Grotto, who were talking next to a jet pack, and said, "Hey, guys! How's it going? And what's this contraption?" "Surpri-se!!!!," they shouted. "It's for you, to, well, you know….," said Fiba. "Well, I was thinking…I was selfish, but then I realized that we are three of the best pirate teams in the goshdarn world! So, keep it!," said Grotto with teary eyes. "You guys…," I said with open arms as I came to them to hug them. "You didn't have to do this for me." "TELL THAT TO THE NORTH POLE!!!," Grotto said. "You saved us! You deserve it,"

Fiba said. "Let's go back to our quarters and celebrate," I said. Maybe it's not good for you, but it's still real to me, darnit!

We came back to our quarters, had fun, watched TV and celebrated. That is, until Dee and Dumber came by and did the most horrible thing unimaginable. Mary quickly cut the cable to the TV and said afterward, "Excuse me but isn't it too soon for you to get brain rot?" I backed away from her, saying, "No, ma'am…" I was 10 levels ahead of Grotto. He was at 35 and Fiba at 25. Then Shelly went up to Fiba and said to her, "You're selected," and Fiba said, "Yes, ma'am," and then Shelly said, "Just kidding…," got out her gun and shot Fiba in the forehead and killed her. MY GIRL!!!!!!! I HOPE SHE STAYS IN SCHOOL FOREVER, THAT JACKALOPE!!!!! WAIT UNTIL I HEAR ABOUT WHAT THE OTHER LITTLE SPIT HAS TO SAY!!!!!!! "AHHHHHHHHH!!!!!!!!!!," screamed Grottoly as he shuddered. "Ooh, we got a live one! Let's interrogate him!," Mary said to Shelly while pinning me against my bed with a sword against me. Then Shelly asked Grottoly in a frilly voice, "Why are you afraid of us?" "THAT'S NOT HOW YOU TREAT YOUR COMRADES!!!!," he uttered while backing away, sobbing and shaking. Within a quick slash of her sword, Shelly cut his head clean off of his neck and toyed with it by making it look like he was saying, "Sorry, I didn't know that you were a Quartermaster," and then mocking him in the middle of it. THE NERVE OF IT ALL!!!!! I'LL KILL HER!!!! I'LL KILL HER IF I WOULD!!!!!! AND THEY GIGGLED AND LAUGHED ABOUT IT!!!!! Then they looked onto me. And Mary said to me, "We heard you told the Captain on those troublesome kids and made us retreat!" She backed away and swung her sword once in fury. "We are pirates!" And she was getting even more mad while looking several ways across the back of her as Shelly asked her, "Mary, what's wrong?," and said, "And if that machine over there is…," and she got even madder. And she looked all over the back of her as Shelly asked her, "What?" Next, Mary pointed her sword at me violently and said in a suddenly rude, but calm manner, "...an escape route." They ran the other way as Mary said, "Prepare to meet us at eleven," without trying to listen to anything make a sound. MY FRIENDS!!!!!!!! YOU MURDERED THEM ALL!!!!! I COULD SEE IF IT WAS THOSE DARN BLOODY KIDS! BUT THEY WENT TOO FAR!!!! THAT'S BETRAYAL!!!! BUT YOU KNOW WHAT?? TO HECK WITH THEIR PRETTY PRETTY PRINCESS DREAMS!!! HERE'S MY BETRAYAL!!!!!

So, I grabbed a backpack as angrily as I could. Took all of my game design notes and supplies into it. Then, in a rage while the ship was going to take off from its spot, I fled to the cargo bay, strapped on the backpack, fitted on the jet pack, opened the hatch to the cargo bay and jetted out of there in a flash. Once I was done, I was now finally on Country B taking janitor jobs. NOW THEY CAN PUT THAT IN THEIR TWIN TAILPIPES AND SMOKE THEM!!!!!!!!

6 years later, I successfully made $1m with my company's latest video game hit, Barrel Stacker! I was even signing deals with Jazzblo on a board game version. A few moments later, some of my retired Card Pirate brethren told me the entire crew was defeated by some ticked off kids thinking they were saving the world. Bless those kids. And they deserve some good old-fashioned shuteye. Rest well my heroes. If it weren't for your meddling, I would have never escaped that life and lived to tell

this tale. **THE END.**

Theater Epilogue

Now, I suppose you were questioning all along about why I wasn't doing any more evil. The thing didn't cross my mind. And as I was jotting down some notes, I fully embraced what they were telling me. I didn't need some dreams, a beauty or some relic to make my dreams come true or to love the world. All I needed was to be good to whatever, or whoever, really guided me here. And I'm not just talking about the stage wright and makeup artist. We run on the guy. And that guy loves us.

Sheesh, it's getting late….Have a good one. And remember to always play out the role the dream gave ya…

Side Chapters

Chapter EXSQ1: Behind a Shield of Rubber

You know, back when I was with my pirate crew, I remembered a few of my crew mates tackling to kill some tree waving wildly about. It didn't catch the Captain's attention until many of us began to fight it in surging numbers. "What is this commotion?," big lard pants asked one of us. And I remember it like a sitcom cutaway dream…

One moment, some of us were beginning to cook in the jungle, until a boulder with a tree other than the one we started fighting after this event flew over us. And we suddenly stared at the darn culprit! And we continued to cook in disbelief, until a pebble hit the ground near a crew mate, that crew mate got distracted by the pebble, and when he investigated, a fat, confused squirrel flew over us and collapsed, recovered and left angry, and we got distracted at that until a tree with a pink rose branch set and a boulder attached to it flew over us, and we looked at that tree, saw the recently-etched words by a tree, "Call Me," were put on it. Judging by the trajectory of the scenery being thrown, either it has to be a rabbit cleaning house or that dang wacky tree. We sent a crew mate to kill whatever's out there, but that tree came up with smart alec responses. Crew mate after crew mate stabbed it and got hammered back in the way it was stabbed. When one grabbed it, it began to lift him in the air, leaving him to drop without it catching, and when we ran from it, it flailed forward and raked us back in range with its wacky branches. As many of us began crying for help, more crew members chimed in on the battle. Now it began to be an all-out war against the inflatable tree!

As the Captain came towards the tree, and after looking at the area in a battle stance and said, "So, you're looking for funk, huh? Well, not in this neck of the woods!," dodged and attacked it like a little, green space goblin with a beam saber, raised his sword in the air and said, "Men! It's time we show it who's the better lover on the street!," aimed his sword at the tree and we all attacked it as an army when he said, "Charge!!!!!"

We made slicing, clamp trap, arrow and gun attacks, but they all bounced off of it. It attacked with its branches in combos every turn it got. Only the poison and dream powder traps seem to weaken its "hide." When we destroyed some of it after that, it flailed more madly and began to lift members out of the area, which was good, since it seemingly wanted to "snug." Enough damage to it provoked to only lift members out of the area, and we're good to go after we all landed on the S.S. Nutting.

The Captain guffawed, then wiped tears of laughter, as he said, "We finally showed him!" "When you said we're better lovers on the street, captain, do you mean it?," he got asked by a crew mate. "HECK NO!!!!," the cap shouted as he shot him dead. To be honest, I was willing to ask him that... "BACK TO WORK!!!!," he said, and boy, did we make one heck of a big punch card.

Chapter EXSQ2: The Timonkey Cometh

You know, back when I was with the pirate crew, I remembered going through the jungle of Semi Cotta with the Captain on our way to pick up Ras from that amusement park she's been going to, until we heard one of those cat monkey things scream out loud in a horrible death kind of way from a faraway setting. "Huh?", the Captain thought as he remained alert, and there were sounds of a large and fast moving object rustling scenery. We kept our guard, until out of nowhere came a big, hulking, tiger-ape abomination, carrying a huge tree as we backed away from it in awe and fear and jumped over the tree as it swung it and declared a hunt!!! "Fight it at once!!!!," the half-torso-misshapen mutant shouted as we all fought it right away.

We dodged huge tree after huge tree of tiger monkey swings, ape-hybrid-made earthquakes and out muscled ape Mun solos being done on random crew members, but it remained on the attack. So we kept trapping until it was weak enough for us to overpower it in constant attacks while it was kept still in one place. After enough attacks, it rebounded all further attacks, roared and then took off. Now I know how those kids would feel if they would go through it. Thinking of it, that'd make kind of a good match! That'll rest them! Unless the bee thing goes full flasher or whatever! Then I'm really scared!!!

As we regrouped, we wondered what the heck that was. "If that thing goes after the ship, I'm killing it," the Captain raised. And we fought a clown kid on the way to, uh-uh-uh-uh! Not telling you that! We picked up Ras and left straight for the ship.

About the Author

Urie Wilson is an entry-level graphics designer, gamer, programmer, animator and avid writer from Chicago who is disabled. He failed to reveal what he knew about his unknown past, yet thinks he can prepare for the future, where he will have to tell everyone the truth about it.

Urie graduated from elementary school, high school, and vocational school(CCG) and dropped out of college when plenty of factors played into it. He is now recovering from it.

Promo

Buy Cori and the Hidden World!

When Going Home is Somewhat Not Happening, Captain!

A country shaped like an A? Air pirates? A legendary relic?

A little boy named Cori had a farm. And he was living the good life, until he accidentally fell into a hole in a barn that suddenly changed everything. With a Light Ghost princess named Bleuelle, who rules the world he is now on, and a robot software bee humanoid engaged to her named Phoe, who is the most comical living vaccine to life, can he save the new world he is on and safely get back home?

- 17 main chapters + 15 side chapters
- Semi-customize-able story
- A setting in a play, filled with monsters and twists relatively imaginable and unforgettable characters
  Now on Amazon and Kindle!

LCCN: 2023919997
Hardcover($16.99): ISBN#979-8-9891283-0-3
Ebook($8.99): ISBN#979-8-9891283-1-0

www.ingramcontent.com/pod-product-compliance
Lightning Source LLC
Chambersburg PA
CBHW020051310726
48970CB00007B/2515